For Serena

Published in the United States, Great Britain, Canada, Australia and New Zealand
in 1988 by North-South Books, an imprint of Nord-Süd Verlag, AG.
First paperback edition published in 1995.
Distributed in the United States by North-South Books, Inc., New York

Library of Congress Cataloging in Publication Data
de Beer, Hans
Ahoy there, little polar bear
Translation of: Kleiner Eisbär, komm bald wieder!
1. Polar Bears—Fiction I. Title
PZ7.D353Li 1987 [E] 88-42533

British Library Cataloguing in Publication Data
Beer, Hans de, 1957-
Ahoy There, Little Polar Bear
I. Title II. Kleiner Eisbär, komm bald wieder. *English.*
833'.914[J]

ISBN 1-55858-028-X (trade binding)
7 9 11 13 15 TB 14 12 10 8 6
ISBN 1-55858-240-1 (library binding)
1 3 5 7 9 LB 10 8 6 4 2
ISBN 1-55858-389-0 (paperback)
1 3 5 7 9 PB 10 8 6 4 2
Printed in Belgium

Ask your bookseller for these
other North-South books by Hans de Beer:

Little Polar Bear
Little Polar Bear, A Pop-Up Book
Little Polar Bear and the Brave Little Hare
Little Polar Bear Finds a Friend
Bernard Bear's Amazing Adventure
Meet the Molesons by Burny Bos
More From the Molesons by Burny Bos
Ollie the Elephant by Burny Bos
On the Road with Poppa Whopper
by Marianne Busser and Ron Schröder

Ahoy There, Little Polar Bear

Written and Illustrated by

Hans de Beer

North-South Books
New York

Lars, the little polar bear, lived with his mother and father near the North Pole where everything was white for as far as the eye could see.

Although he spent much of his time alone, he was happy.

But one day, when Lars swam quite far from his den, something terrible happened. Lars caught his foot, was pulled down deep into the sea, then yanked up in a gigantic net.

Lars was dropped to the ground with such a bang, he fainted. When he awoke he couldn't tell where he was. Above him was a ladder, so he climbed up the slippery rungs.

Lars roamed the long hallways. It seemed he was all alone until something rustled behind him. As he turned around two large eyes stared at him. Lars ran for his life.

Just when he thought he was safe again, he heard a voice: "Don't be afraid. It's only me, Nemo, the ship's cat. Welcome aboard."

Lars looked up. Above him was a friendly looking creature with orange fur. Lars could see that Nemo was an animal he could trust.

"I'm Lars," said the little polar bear. "I'm trying to get home as soon as I can."

"I'm afraid that isn't possible, at least not right away," Nemo said. "Your home is a long way from where we are now."

"Where are we?" asked Lars.

"We're on a ship, on our way back to port. Once we're there I'll take you to see some friends who may be able to help. But until then there isn't anything we can do. Why don't we get something to eat? I expect you're very hungry."

When he had eaten, Lars felt much more cheerful. He curled up beside Nemo and fell fast asleep.

When they awoke, Nemo took Lars up to the deck. "Look," he said, pointing to the horizon, which was aglow with lights. "That's the port. We'll be there soon."

Lars was so excited he could hardly wait to go ashore. When the ship had come into port Lars eagerly followed Nemo onto the deck and over the plank.

"Try to look inconspicuous," said Nemo.

What Lars found on the other side of the plank surprised and disappointed him. Everything was so untidy and dirty.

"I'm afraid this isn't a very clean place," sighed Nemo. "We'd best hurry. Follow me around the back way. The streets are much too dangerous."

As Lars and Nemo made their way through alleys and back streets, Lars's white coat became dirtier and dirtier. He wished more than ever that he was home again, where everything was clean and white.

Following Nemo over fences and along walls took all Lars's efforts.

At last Nemo stopped.

"We have arrived," he announced. "Wait here a moment."

It was very dark. Many eyes were staring at Lars. He grew quite nervous.

But the eyes belonged to some more cats who turned out to be just as friendly as Nemo.

The cats looked grave as Nemo explained Lars's problem. They thought it over for a few minutes. Then a black and white cat stepped forward. "I'm Johnny, also a ship's cat," he said. "My ship is leaving for the Arctic tomorrow. We must get you on board before daylight."

Lars, Johnny and Nemo had to rush back through the alleys and backyards. Lars was so excited to be on his way home again, he forgot to watch where he was going and was almost hit by a truck.

When Lars reached the ship he said good bye to Nemo quickly, for there was not much time. It was a sad moment.

For Lars, the time on the ship passed quickly. It wasn't long before, he spotted something wonderful on the horizon. "Look Johnny!" he shouted. "The North Pole. See how clean and white it is. I was once as clean and white as that."

That night, when the ship anchored, Lars thanked Johnny and set off for the beautiful white shores of the North Pole.

As Lars swam, the sea washed his fur clean. Once on shore, Lars ran for his den to greet his worried parents, who couldn't have been happier to see him. When Lars told his parents about his adventures, their mouths dropped open.

"And this is what Nemo looks like," Lars explained as he tried his best to look like a cat. Although his parents were not sure they understood, they were so happy to have Lars home again it didn't really matter. That night they all slept close together.

After that day, Lars's father often found his son gazing out at the horizon. "What are you looking for?" he asked.

"Ships," Lars said. "And cats too. Some day a cat might fall off a ship and come to visit us."